HERCULES THE YOUNGER

Kathryn James

Illustrated by **Oliver Averill**

UNIVERSITY PRESS

I've been happily writing books for children and teenagers for many years.

Before becoming a writer, my favourite job was working with Gypsy and Traveller children – running arts and crafts classes from a converted bus with a big rainbow on the side! It was the most fun I've ever had at work. I've even written several books about the children and teenagers I met on the bus.

When I'm not writing, I spend time in Manchester with my family and little grandaughters. I enjoy weekends in North Wales, walking on the beach with the family dog, or in the Clwyd hills, enjoying the peace and quiet – if only the dog would stop barking at squirrels.

Kathryn James

Mum held up the bent pushchair wheel. 'Hercules!' she yelled. 'Did you do this?'

Hercules Young tried to look innocent. Unfortunately, it didn't work.

'I was trying to fix the pushchair,' he explained.

Mum sighed. 'I wish you wouldn't.'

His dad held up a pair of his waterproof trousers. 'Please stop filling my fishing trousers full of sand, and using them as a punchbag, Hercules! You've punched right through them!'

Hercules just didn't know his own strength. When he was a baby, he would bite right through his picture books.

Once, he bounced so high that he almost leaped right out of the baby bouncer! That's why his parents named him after his great-great-great-grandfather, Hercules the First.

Hercules the First was a circus strongman. He had a curly moustache and a leopard-print leotard.

He travelled around the country, performing amazing acts of strength. His most daring trick was catching a cannonball fired out of a real cannon!

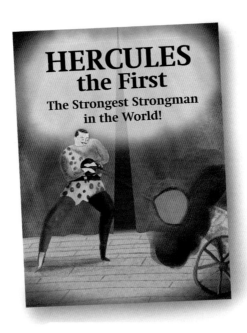

Nowadays, the Youngs still travelled around the country. Hercules loved sitting outside with his grandad, hearing stories about his super-strong ancestor.

'I bet one day you'll entertain the crowds, too,' said Grandad. 'You're Hercules the Younger!'

Hercules liked the sound of that, but right now he was lonely. His cousins wouldn't play with him because he accidentally broke their toys. His sisters were too young. And his older brothers were always out at work with Dad, in his motor.

'It's time for your boxing class, Hercules,' said Mum. 'Let's hope you don't break anything there!' she smiled.

All the Youngs loved boxing. Hercules hoped he'd be a champion one day. But when he got to the gym, none of the children in his class wanted to train with him. He was too strong, they said.

Hercules's Uncle Pete ran the gym. Uncle Pete held up his hand and said, 'Let's see how hard you can punch.'

Hercules threw his best punch. Uncle Pete gasped and shook his hand. 'You need to go into the top class, Herc.'

The children in the top class were much older than Hercules. They didn't want to hang around with younger kids. When the class finished, they all went off without him.

One day I'll be famous, thought Hercules as he watched them leave. *Then everyone will want to be my friend.*

The next day at school, things didn't get off to a good start. Hercules made a clay bowl in Art class. But when he put it on the display table, he managed to tip the whole thing over. Pottery slid in all directions and crashed to the floor.

'Oops!' he said as his classmates groaned.

'You don't know your own strength,' sighed his teacher, Mr Malik. 'Try to be more careful.'

'I will,' Hercules promised. And then forgot.

When the class marched to the hall for assembly, Herc was daydreaming about being a champion boxer, and barged straight into Zoya. She went flying. He said sorry, but Zoya looked at him like he was a galumphing elephant. She avoided him after that.

At lunchtime, Hercules joined Oskar's football game in the playground. When Oskar kicked the ball to Hercules, Hercules kicked it back.

'Oops!' he said, as the ball soared into the sky, disappearing over the roof.

Oskar scowled. 'What did you do that for?'

'I didn't mean to,' said Hercules.

Oskar didn't talk to him again all day.

The next morning, Mr Malik said, 'It's time for our nature ramble. We're going to do our minibeast survey.' He glanced out of the window. 'Last night's storm has cleared up, so we can go outside. Wellies on, everyone!'

When they reached the woods, they had to get into teams. Hercules looked around. Everyone had joined a team except Oskar and Zoya. 'You three can work together,' said Mr Malik.

Hercules beamed at them. 'This is going to be fun,' he exclaimed. Oskar scowled as they set off together.

He didn't want Hercules ruining things again. Zoya kept her distance so Hercules couldn't knock her over. They splashed through puddles and then found a couple of blown-down trees. The roots were a good place to look for minibeasts.

Hercules and Zoya started searching the tangled roots of one tree.

'This one looks better!' Oskar shouted, and he started running towards the other tree.

He was too excited to notice the muddy patch in front of it.

'Whoops!' Oskar shouted, as his feet began to slide faster and faster. He waved his arms, trying to keep his balance, but his feet went flying and he hit the ground.

'Help!' he howled.

Hercules and Zoya ran and found Oskar sitting beside the fallen tree.

'What's wrong?' said Zoya.

'My welly's trapped under the tree trunk!' Oskar groaned.

'Can't you wriggle it out?' said Hercules.

Oskar tried. 'No! It's stuck.'

'I'll go and get Mr Malik,' said Zoya, and she ran off at high speed.

'Let me try to pull out your foot,' said
Hercules. He bent down and tugged
Oskar's welly.

'Ow!' cried Oskar.

'Hmm, that's not going to work. You're
really stuck,' said Hercules. 'I'll have to
lift the tree.'

'You can't lift a tree!' said Oskar.

'I can try,' said Hercules.

He bent his knees and put his hands under the tree trunk. Then he pulled upwards as hard as he could but nothing happened. The tree was so heavy! He nearly gave up but then he thought of Hercules the First. His great-great-great-grandfather would have easily picked up the tree.

I can do this, thought Hercules. He took hold of the trunk again and braced his knees. Then he gave a huge roar and heaved with all his might. This time the tree lifted straight up into the air!

Oskar quickly scrambled free. 'You did it!' he shouted, hopping about.

As Hercules carefully lowered the tree, Mr Malik and Zoya came running, followed by the rest of the class.

'Hercules lifted up the tree and saved my toes!' Oskar explained happily.

Mr Malik and the class gasped.

Zoya ran over to Hercules. 'That was really brave!' she told him.

'Thanks, Herc,' said Oskar, grinning.

Everyone was amazed at Hercules's strength. His knees were shaking but he struck a strongman pose and made them all laugh.

When they got back to the class,
Hercules told everyone about his great-
great-great-grandfather, Hercules the
First. There were gasps as he described
the cannonball trick.

Oskar put up his hand. 'What else
could he do?'

'Lots of incredible things,' said
Hercules. 'I've got old photos to prove it.'

'Why don't you, Oskar and Zoya do a presentation about Hercules the First for the end-of-term assembly?' said Mr Malik.

'Yes!' they agreed.

That week, Hercules invited Oskar and Zoya over to look at the old and precious photos of Hercules the First.

'I like the one of him folding a frying pan in half,' said Zoya.

'I like the one of him lifting a huge boulder,' said Oskar.

Hercules's favourite was the photo of the strongman catching a cannonball.

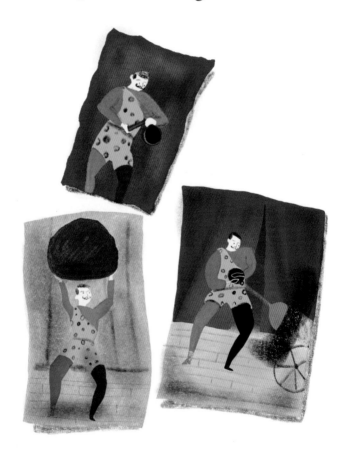

'Hmm. I've got an idea,' said Hercules, with a grin. 'We could do our own strongman show at the end of the presentation.'

'Brilliant!' agreed Oskar.

'I'll make the props!' said Zoya.

When the end-of-term assembly came, their strongman presentation was a massive success. Zoya groaned as she folded a cardboard frying pan. Oskar pretended his knees were trembling as he lifted a papier mâché boulder over his head. Finally, a plastic cannonball flew across the stage as Zoya and Oskar shouted 'BOOM!'

'Ooph!' said Hercules, as he caught it.

BOOM!

Hercules grinned as the audience cheered. *I'm definitely Hercules the Younger now*, he thought. *And best of all, I've got amazing friends!*